# Vagnarok Finds a Sweetheart

**Written by** John Parsons
**Illustrated by** Peter Shaw

## Contents

NELSON
CENGAGE Learning™
For learning solutions, visit **cengage.com.au**

# Meet the Characters

**Vagnarok**

A badly behaved Viking chief.

**Horrid**

A female Viking warrior.

**Torrid**

A Viking warrior.

**Gryme**

A Viking poet.

**Other Viking villagers**

Male and female Vikings.

Dear Reader

Here's another fun play featuring all your favourite badly behaved Viking characters! This time, the Viking men find themselves in a bit of a pickle. They smell, are naughty and have rather unpleasant habits.

But for some reason, the girl Vikings don't want to be their dates for an important ball. I wonder why?

John Parsons

Author

## The Viking Village

1. The fjord

2 & 3. Viking girls live here

4 & 5. Viking boys live here

6. The cooking pot

# 1 The Characters

You will need the following characters:

## NARRATOR

The Narrator is the character telling the story of the conundrum facing the Vikings. The narrator, responsible for setting the scene for the audience and recounting episodes of the story so everyone understands what's going on, is positioned on one side of the stage and may be a girl or a boy or even a teacher.

## VAGNAROK

Vagnarok is a fearsome and ferocious Viking chief who is rather untidy and misbehaves quite a lot – but underneath all the fearsomeness and ferocity, Vagnarok has a good heart, and he is secretly worried about what everyone thinks of him!

## GRYME

Gryme is different from the other Vikings, because he thinks there are better things to do than waggling swords and swinging battle axes at each other. In fact, he is rather reluctant to fight at all, preferring instead to spend his time and talents waggling and swinging his pen, writing long poems called sagas about the other Vikings and their deeds.

## TORRID

Torrid is one of Vagnarok's fearsome Vikings. He is a typical Viking who speaks loudly and with a deep voice, and feels much more comfortable waving a sword when he speaks!

## HORRID

Horrid is also one of Vagnarok's fearsome Vikings. Her favourite accessory is a battleaxe, which she is very experienced at swinging (while everyone else ducks), and she is rather overbearing.

## KING BLØDENGUTS

King Blødenguts, whose name is pronounced "blood 'n' guts", lives in the next town and is the undisputed ruler of all the Vikings. He doesn't have a speaking part, but could sit on the side of the stage observing the action.

## OTHER VIKINGS

The other Vikings can be boys or girls. There is one essential qualification for being a fearsome and ferocious Viking: you must pull a frighteningly horrible face when you say "Eeeew!" You may also wear a long, straggly, whiskery beard, but this is optional. If you haven't got one already, or you are a girl, you can make an artificial one using paper.

# 2 The Props

To be convincing Vikings, you will need the following props:

- Sufficient cardboard swords for everyone (be careful that they aren't too pointy because Vikings with eye patches will encounter difficulties reading their scripts properly)
- A cardboard battleaxe (be careful that the edges aren't too sharp because Vikings without all their fingers and toes will encounter difficulties turning the pages properly)
- Viking costumes (a dirty one and a clean one with a flower for Vagnarok)
- Paper beards for those who want them (be careful that they don't look too realistic, otherwise sparrows, crows or Norwegian arctic foxes might build their nests in them)

- A supply of colourful towels (if you can't find Viking towels made of reindeer wool or polar bear whiskers, ordinary ones will do)
- A classroom-sized collection of buckets and mops or brooms (hollowed-out mammoth skulls and birch brooms work best, but plastic ones will do).

# 3 The Script

NARRATOR:

*(With a bold and booming theatrical voice, used alongside generous arm-waving and melodramatic flourishes.)*

Now listen to this saga
Of Vagnarok the Vile.
Attracting ladies, he found out,
Required a change of style.

He hardly ever brushed his teeth,
Or washed between his toes.
He used old socks to wash his face,
His sleeve to wipe his nose.

No better were his Viking friends,
A smelly, stinking crew!
Whenever they turned up for tea,
The ladies all said ...

PICKLED
HERRINGS

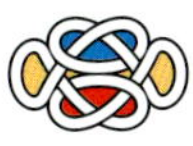

ALL GIRL VIKINGS:

*(All together, screwing up their faces and sounding doubly disgusted and rather revolted.)*

Pooh!

VAGNAROK:

*(With a puzzled and bewildered voice.)*

I don't know what you're complaining about! I brush my hair with sardine grease every day, and every night I turn my underpants inside out before I go to sleep on my compost heap.

OTHER VIKINGS:

*(All together, holding their noses.)*

Eeeew!

**NARRATOR:**

Among the band of Vikings lived
a poet they called Gryme.
Instead of swinging swords about,
He loved his words to rhyme.

One day, an invitation came
Which Gryme did read out loud.
And with each word, came hearty claps
And cheering from the crowd.

**HORRID:**

*(Cupping a hand near her mouth and speaking sideways to the audience.)*

Until the last line!

GRYME:

*(Reading from a scroll.)*

A royal invitation is
Extended to you all.
King Blødenguts is getting hitched
There'll be a wedding ball.

The party starts at half past six.
He warns us, don't be late!
His new queen, Odourina, says
We all must bring a date!

ALL GIRL VIKINGS:

*(All together, clapping in excitement.)*

A wedding ball! Hurrah!

ALL BOY VIKINGS:

*(Looking glum.)*

A date! Oh, no!

TORRID:

You mean we have to actually find girls who will go on a date with us?

VAGNAROK:

*(With a horrified voice.)*

That can't be right! Let me look at that invitation.

*(Reads invitation, then nods sadly to the boy Vikings, who all groan loudly.)*

NARRATOR:

Poor Vagnarok and all his men,
their ladies had to please.
They blew them slurpy kisses that
Smelled like stinky cheese.

With smelly breath and filthy clothes,
They didn't have a clue
The ladies all responded with
A loud resounding ...

ALL GIRL VIKINGS:

Eeeew!

HORRID:

*(Folding her arms.)*

If you think we are going to be your dates, there will have to be some changes around here. I'm not going anywhere with anyone who smells like a dead walrus or who looks like they've woken up in a pigsty!

TORRID:

*(Enthusiastically.)*

Actually, if you smell like a dead walrus, I find the pigs leave you alone. It's the blowflies that wake you up.

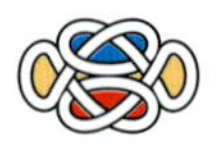

GRYME:

*(Scratching his chin thoughtfully.)*

I sense there is some discontent
Amongst our lady friends.
We need to make ourselves ship-shape,
We need to make amends.

We Vikings aren't romantic.
Sweet petals we are not.
Let's rack our brains and find a way
To make ourselves look hot!

VAGNAROK:

*(Sniffing his armpits and nodding proudly.)*

I've always found that shovelling horse dung out of the stables makes me feel quite warm and sweaty. We could all do that!

HORRID:

*(Shaking her head.)*

So far, that's not working for me. Maybe you could start by using this.

*(Hands Vagnarok a bar of soap.)*

## NARRATOR:

The challenge that the Vikings faced
Made each man scratch his head.
They shrugged their shoulders, frowned a lot
They tossed and turned in bed.

They needed to impress their dates.
"But how?" thought Vagnarok.
He stretched and yawned and picked his nose
Then rubbed it with a sock.

He chewed his toenails, cleaned his ears
With belly-button fluff.
"Impressing girls, I never thought
That it would be so tough."

**HORRID:**

*(Walking past.)*

Morning, Vagnarok. Did you sleep well?

**VAGNAROK:**

*(Rubbing his belly.)*

No, that block of cheese you gave me yesterday tasted awful. I spent all night burping bubbles.

**TORRID:**

*(Rushes up to Vagnarok.)*

I have an idea. Let's charm the ladies by cooking dinner for them. They'll think we're ever so sweet and they will all want to be our dates for King Blødenguts' wedding ball.

SOAP

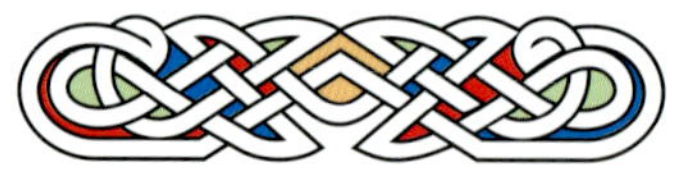

VAGNAROK:

*(Excitedly.)*

Good thinking, Torrid. That will impress them. And when they see what good cooks we are, they will all want to come to the ball with us!

NARRATOR:

A feast to win the ladies!
Perhaps their hearts would thaw?
Alas, alack, for Vagnarok,
The plan did have a flaw.

Of Viking culinary skills,
The best that can be said
Was most of the ingredients
Were thankfully quite dead.

Fish eyes, crab guts, crunchy snails
Toss 'em in, the lot.
A squirming worm, a slimy slug
Toss 'em in the pot.

Some stinging nettles and a toad
Some toenails add some spice.
A thistle, if it's handy
Can be really rather nice!

Stir that mixture, scrape the sides
Boil that bubbling mix.
And if it needs a little crunch
Throw in some celery sticks.

Your guests, when they do taste it
Will love this hearty stew
We guarantee the words they'll say are ...

ALL GIRL VIKINGS:

*(Wrinkling their noses in disgust.)*

Pooh! Pooh! POOH!

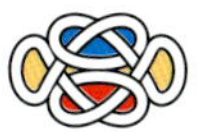

TORRID:

*(Pleased.)*

I think they like it! I hope there's some leftovers for breakfast!

**NARRATOR:**

Alas, the ladies hurried by,
The men still had no dates.
They shrugged their shoulders, rolled their eyes
And went to get their plates.

**HORRID:**

***(From a distance.)***

Poor Vagnarok, you've got it wrong
You've clearly no idea.
If you'd like to ask us out
I'll make this very, very clear.

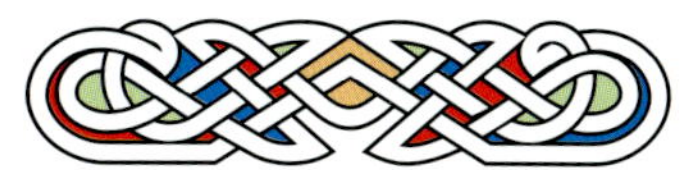

To ask a lady on a date
You have to show respect
To brush your teeth and take a bath
Is the least she will expect.

You need to be a gentleman
You need to make her smile
If you ask her to eat that smelly slop
She'll surely run a mile.

ALL GIRL VIKINGS:

We'd like our dates to listen
We'd like our dates to care
We'd like our dates to first remove
The weevils in their hair.

If you asked us nicely
And promised to behave
If you learned good manners
And tried to have a shave.

If you washed your underpants
And scrubbed between your toes
If you promised not to burp
Then asked us, well, who knows?

Smarten up, that's all we ask
Behave yourselves, that's all
We might say yes and be your dates
at Blødenguts's ball.

VAGNAROK:

*(Looking alarmed.)*

Listening? Caring? Behaving? Washing? And no burping? Whatever next?

## ALL BOY VIKINGS:

We're rough and tumble Viking men
It's hard to change our ways
We've been working on our smell
For days and days and days.

We like our filthy fingernails
Our bad breath makes us proud
And most of all, when we burp
We like to burp out loud!

We never wash behind our ears,
We hate the smell of soap
For us to get a date, it seems,
There really is no hope.

## GRYME:

In the search for sweethearts
The Vikings did seem doomed.
It seemed they must rethink their ways
Before a romance bloomed.

The thought of that was daunting
The prospect was quite scary.
'Cos Viking men, they loved to be
Smelly, rude and hairy.

But still, their ruler Blødenguts
Insisted they bring dates
The poor defeated Vikings were
Resigned to their fates.

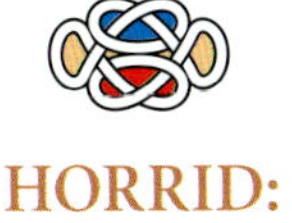

HORRID:

*(Triumphantly.)*

Bring those scissors, bring that soap
That book of etiquette
Soon our men will be the smoothest
Blokes we've ever met.

***(Horrid and the girl Vikings shuffle together to form a circle around Vagnarok and the boy Vikings, holding up towels so the audience can't see what's going on.)***

A sprinkling of good manners,
A dose of thoughtfulness
A clip, a scrub, a shave and then
We ladies might say yes.

VAGNAROK:

*(In a frightened voice.)*

Help! Help!

ALL BOY VIKINGS:

Ouch! Ooh! Aargh!

TORRID:

I hope you ladies are going to shave your whiskers too! Ouch!

## NARRATOR:

Teeth were scrubbed, eyebrows trimmed
Beards, they were removed.
The ladies worked and worked until ...

## ALL GIRL VIKINGS:

Our men, they have improved!

*(The circle formed by Horrid and the girl Vikings parts to reveal a line of angelic, clean Vikings standing like a row of choirboys. Each holds a small book from which he reads.)*

ALL BOY VIKINGS:

The Viking *Guide to Ladies*
Turn to chapter one.
Don't misbehave, curse or burp
That's not the way it's done.

VAGNAROK:

*(Stage whisper.)*

How long will Blødenguts's ball be? I have a feeling it could be a long, long night!

ALL BOY VIKINGS:

The Viking *Guide to Ladies*
Turn to chapter two.
If you'd like to find a date
Then this is what you do.

**TORRID:**

That can't be right! Are you sure this is going to work?

**VAGNAROK:**

It must be a spelling mistake. It says give them a flower. I would have thought a fish-head would have been more useful.

**HORRID:**

*(Shaking her head.)*

Men. They just won't read the instructions.

GRYME:

The Vikings held their roses up
Then all fell to their knees.
"Courage, men!" said Vagnarok.
Then they all smiled – "Cheese!"

*(Vagnarok, Torrid and the boy Vikings all say "cheese" and hold a broad stage-grin.)*

NARRATOR:

Lashes fluttered, ladies swooned
They blushed and all looked coy.
Then every Viking lady went
And chose a Viking boy.

*(All the Vikings pair off,*
*except for Vagnarok and Horrid,*
*who look shyly at each other.)*

VAGNAROK:

Horrid, I've always been quite impressed at the way you swing a battleaxe. And you can poke your tongue out in a way that makes even fearsome Vikings tremble.

HORRID:

Vagnarok, you sweet talker. You sure know the way to a girl's heart.

VAGNAROK:

So, I've been wondering.

HORRID:

Yes?

VAGNAROK:

Well, if you weren't doing anything tomorrow ...

HORRID:

Yes?

VAGNAROK:

Would you be my date for the ball?

HORRID:

Yes!

ALL VIKINGS:

Hurrah!

*(All the Vikings exit stage in pairs,*
*except for Vagnarok and Horrid*
*who are the last to leave.)*

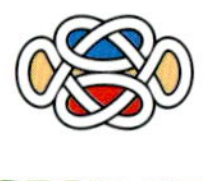

GRYME:

The Vikings went off, two by two
Each happy with their date.
They were all ready for the ball.
They all could hardly wait.

The night would be a great success,
They'd dance until the dawn.
And each man do his very best
Not to burp or yawn.

*(Vagnarok and Horrid hold hands and walk towards exit. They stop.)*

HORRID:

You're not really going to change, are you, Vagnarok?

VAGNAROK:

Highly unlikely, my dear.

HORRID:

That's a relief! Hey, do you want to come and check out my battleaxe collection?

VAGNAROK:

Can I bring my broadswords? I've got a spare fish head, if you fancy a snack!

HORRID:

It's a date!

*(Vagnarok and Horrid exit.)*

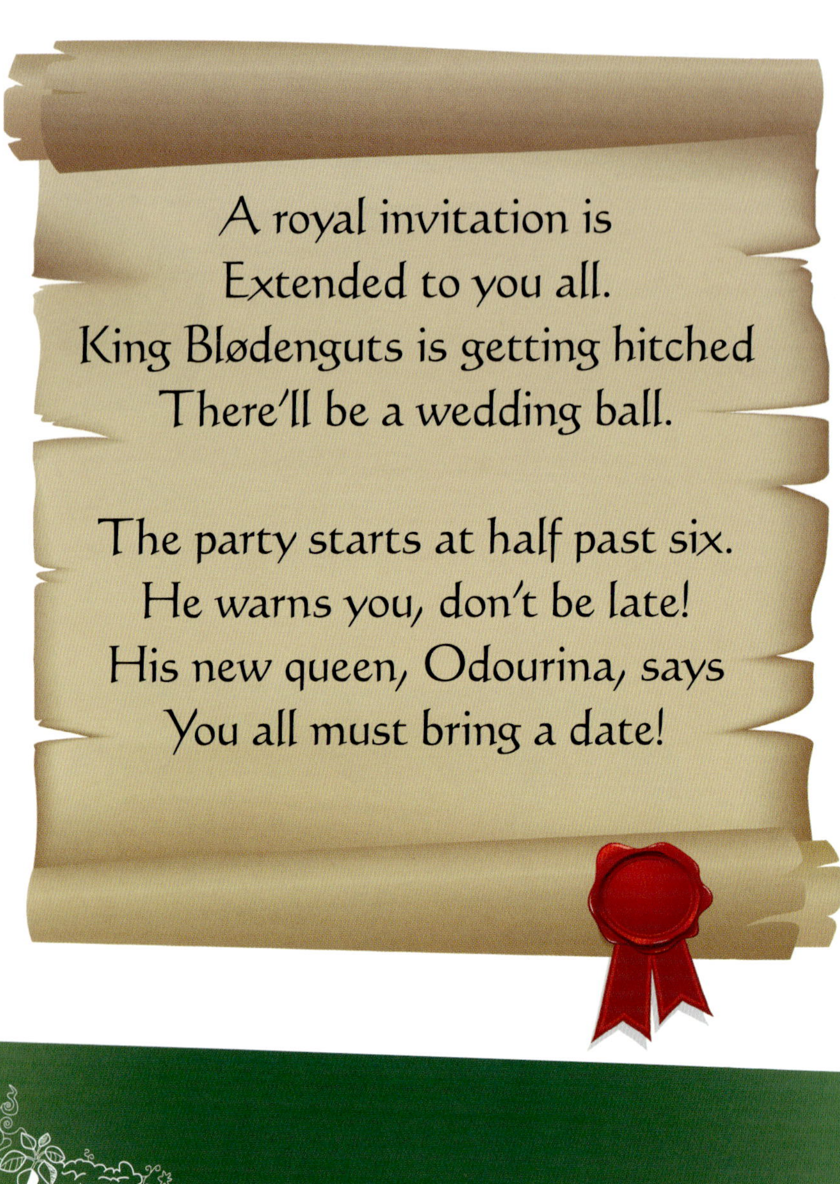
A royal invitation is
Extended to you all.
King Blødenguts is getting hitched
There'll be a wedding ball.

The party starts at half past six.
He warns you, don't be late!
His new queen, Odourina, says
You all must bring a date!